THE
GNOME

THIS IS A PRION BOOK

First published in 2010

This edition published in 2011 by Prion
A division of Carlton Books Limited
20 Mortimer Street
London W1T 3JW

10 9 8 7 6 5 4 3 2 1

A CIP catalogue record for this book is available from the British
Library.

ISBN 978 1 85375 825 6

Publishing Manager: Vanessa Daubney
Project Editor: Jennifer Barr
Creative Director: Clare Baggaley
Design: Ceri Woods
Photography: Russell Porter
Production Controller: Karin Kolbe

Printed in Dubai

Gnomes supplied by The Gnome Reserve and Wildflower Garden
The Gnome Reserve
West Putford
Nr Bradworthy, N Devon
EX22 7XE
tel 01409 241435
fax 08715 227633

http://www.gnomereserve.co.uk

With special thanks to Ann and Richard Atkins.

Joel Jessup has asserted his moral right to be identified as the
author of this book.

THE GNOME

by Joel Jessup

PRION

INTRODUCTION

Belief in natural spirits has existed throughout human history, and people have fashioned representations of creatures such as sprites, imps and the hardy troll using all manner of different materials, from bronze and stone to leftover pieces of chewing gum.

But it's the humble gnome who wins the popular vote. Whereas other forest spirits can appear intimidating – like they might leap out of the bracken and mug you for your pocket change and socks – gnomes are sweet, good natured and couldn't look threatening if they tried.

Despite this, very little is actually known about the lives and habits of gnomes. Where did they come from? Why do they like gardens? And is Santa just an over-sized, freak gnome who happens to prefer a cold climate?

It has been established that gnomes were first spotted towards the end of the nineteenth century in gardens in Gräfenroda, Germany. However, they were probably around for many thousands of years before that but just kept themselves to themselves. There is some speculation that the "modern" gnome is actually a new breed that grew tired of living in forests and fields – understandable, given the difficulty of trying to sleep on scraps of moss while one's long-eared, furry neighbours rabbit on about how great carrots are. But apart from this, there has been no information with any substance on the subject...

Until we stepped up and said, "Enough! We will create the definitive gnome book, no matter if we go insane in the process... no matter if we already have, which is obviously how we came up with the idea in the first place!"

This labour of love is the culmination of years of research and time spent crouching in gardens and flower-beds around the globe. And let's not forget the occasional night in a police cell. We made notes and took photos. We even attempted to conduct a few interviews but received the silent treatment. The result is a fair balance of gnowledge and gnonsense.

Welcome to the book!

My wheelbarrow may look empty
but it contains dreams.

And some termites,
I think.

Gnome Hats

Gnomes across the world sport a pointy hat (or gnome cap), which is the traditional, requisite headgear. Its origins go back four hundred years when gnomes wore special helmets into battle or, if none were available, ice-cream cones. The height of the hat affords a perfect hiding place for snacks – especially heated pies that have the added advantage of keeping heads warm on winter days. The only gnome to deviate from this stylish norm was Sherlock Gnolmes, who was well known for his pointy deer-stalker hat and the catchphrase, "Lift me up, I can't see the blinking crime scene!"

Gnome
Hobbies

Gnomes have many different hobbies, but not necessarily the ones you'd imagine. Most consider fishing, pushing wheelbarrows and chuckling to be their proper day job but in their spare time they like to build small catamarans, play the electric bagpipes or learn to speak Frog. Of course, the most popular gnome pastime is joyriding your lawnmower.

A badger ate the yellow card, so I'm going to use this pork scratching, alright?

12

Goooooooooooaaaaaaalllllllllllll wait, actually I missed.

13

Gnome Confusion

Some gnomes get very confused. The gnome here, for example, is clearly a tractor driver and yet he seems to think it's his job to sell apples to passing squirrels. Maybe their confusion is because gnomes have never quite adjusted to the sparser foliage and brighter light of suburban gardens and are suffering from a form of sunstroke. Some people suggest that wearing pointy hats for thousands of years has created pointy heads with little triangular brains. We asked some gnomes about this but they didn't quite understand what we were talking about.

Go Fish?
I thought we were
playing Blackjack!

How come I'm
down £2,000?

And don't think I can't see
Fred under the table – he's not
exactly Captain Subtle...

17

Must stay alert...

Keep my eye on the ball...
Dedication is everything...
One hundred and ten per cent...

So what if everyone else
packed up and went
home two hours ago?

I'm about three
hundred over par.
But I still think
I might get the
prize for

"Cheekiest Golfer
with the Best Socks".

20

Space Gnomes

A number of gnome experts (or gnomeologists) have mooted the possibility that gnomes may have come from another planet in some kind of toadstool saucer or pointy red rocket. They also suggest possible gnome involvement in the building of the pyramids, given their rather pointy shape. While all this speculation is a bit far-fetched, we can say for certain that gnomes have visited outer space – why else would we have this picture of one wearing a space suit? Ipso facto... gnomeso.

Hey,
foxy gnome lady,
why don't you join me?

22

Hmmm... Ralph needs to get glasses...
That's an actual fox he's talking to.

Gnome Love

Gnomes, like humans, tend to form lifelong monogamous relationships in perfect harmony. OK, maybe more like swans. But before they get together there is the awkward gnome courtship period. Fresh flowers are usually exchanged although nature-loving gnomes refuse to pick them and so just take each other to where they grow. Giving chocolates with mushroom centres makes a good first impression; this can be followed by a walk around a pond or two and - if the mood is right - a little peck on the beard. Alternatively, couples might go paintballing.

GNOME MUSIC

Welcome humans, I'm Gnorbert, and although this may look like a stack of cheese sandwiches it's actually a gnomecordion! Like the human version, it has keys and works by being pumped full of air, but there is one big difference: we gnomes play our instrument using our beards! As you can see, my whiskers have become entwined in the gnomecordian and alter the sound by way of special magical hairs and trained nits! The music is incomparable! It takes a while to get disentangled when I'm done, though.

Meanwhile, Jim over there is playing a tiny guitar. It's not special or anything.

Ignore him.

27

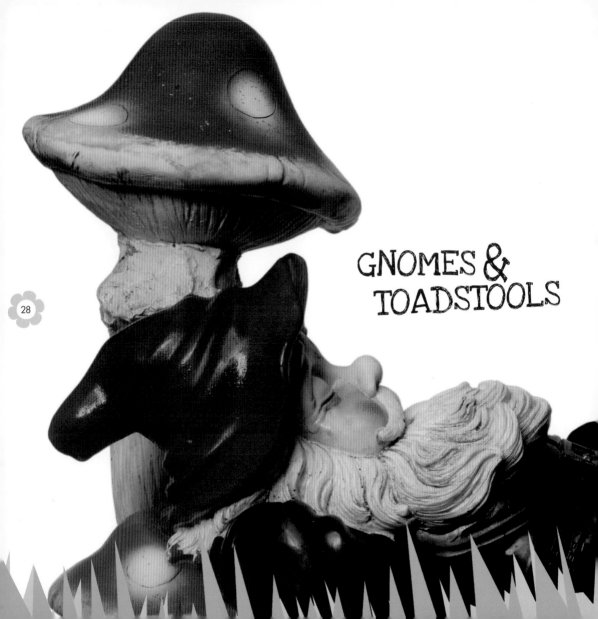

GNOMES &
TOADSTOOLS

Just as dogs adore their masters and tick-picker birds love the rhinos they sit on, So gnomes are fond of toadstools, and vice versa. This pleasant interspecies relationship means that gnomes use toadstools as seats, umbrellas, houses and sometimes – inexplicably – as photocopiers. In return, gnomes keep the toadstools clean and damp and share their food with them. "what, even pizza?" I hear you ask. That I don't know. Another mystery is whether toadstools spring up where gnomes hang out, or if gnomes just follow the toadstool trail. There is always the possibility that they move around in tandem and share the rent and bills.

Ssh! I'm just pretending to be asleep so I don't get roped into playing croquet.

I'm still bruised from last time!

30

Seriously, how cool is this log golf-cart? I made it this morning! Honest!

31

Gnome Technology

Gnomes favour a natural lifestyle so eschew such modern devices as mp3-players, laptops and electric can-openers. But there are a number of more primitive devices that gnomes swear by – for example, the self-opening mechani-gate, the automatic pointy-hat starcher and the aggressive chaffinch scare-awayer. These things are usually powered either by natural water streams or by some strange gnome magic... or AA batteries.

Look, I said I was just going to have two drinks, and that's what I'm doing! Where are those straws?

34

AwWwWwW.

35

Gnome friendship

Obviously all gnomes consider themselves to be part of a large community of friends. But gnomes everywhere have a particular best mate – the one they'll save their favourite jokes for, always ask to go fishing with and use as a signatory if they decide to start up a small business. As gnomes enjoy incredible longevity, these friendships can last for centuries. It's even said that there are two gnomes out there who built Stonehenge together so that they'd have somewhere to store their spare fishing rods.

37

Gnomes don't normally wear camouflage as they want to be as visible as possible but some of them like it just because it's so **fabulous.**

This gnome looks like he's gone in for the camouflage look but actually he just got a load of leaves and mud mixed up with his white wash.

It's difficult doing laundry in a garden...

Gnomes and Wheelbarrows

Gnomes love all types of gardening equipment but they reserve a special place in their hearts for the wheelbarrow. It's ideal for ferrying things around the garden, whether it's food, laundry, friendly insects, other gnomes or items stolen from inside your house (or gnomestead). Wheelbarrows have been part and parcel of gnome life for so long that some people believe they predate the invention of the wheel (in which case they would simply be called "barrows"). The availability of wheelbarrows is the reason gnomes prefer to dwell in gardens.

And So Squippy the accountancy squirrel decided it was time to buy a new calculator! Isn't that interesting, boys and girls?

41

Hi,
I'm Sorry but
I'm feeling a
little sheepish...

Don't worry,

I'm very skilled at hugging and driving at the same time.

OH NO, LOOK OUT!.... Kidding.

GNOME WISDOM

Gnomes are a great source of wise sayings and adages, and they have a lot to teach us if we can be bothered to crouch down in our front gardens and listen to them. They know when the wind will change, the exact moment milk will go off and when it's time to stop wearing f lip-flops. They can name every kind of animal, tree and, for some reason, jet aircraft. Gnomes can even open cardboard milk cartons without showering themselves with the contents. But they keep the mechanics behind that particular trick a secret.

Gnome is where the heart is.

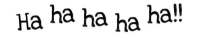

Ha ha ha ha ha!!

You should see the
look on your face!

46

Ignore him,

Oh my goodness...

What's that
up your nose?!?

And this...
is a toadstool!

Have they been mentioned
in the book yet? Yes?

Fine, forget it!

I was just trying to
make conversation...

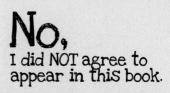

No,
I did NOT agree to appear in this book.

Go away!
I'm shy!

49

Look, it's the first time we met!

I pushed you into the pond and you threw a koi carp at me...

So romantic.

51

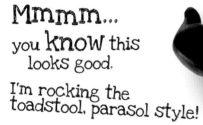

Mmmm...
you **know** this
looks good.

I'm rocking the
toadstool, parasol style!

Gnome Sports

Gnomes prefer garden sports to any other type of competitive physical activity. Croquet is a particular favourite, although for gnomes it usually involves dribbling the ball through the hoops while three others chase after, holding the mallet. They also like tennis, football and garden chess but it takes a while to mow the grass into the chequered pattern. They are partial to golf as well, usually using mole hills for holes, and moles as caddies.

Hey, I got my badger riding licence today!

High five!

55

Not that I'm complaining,
but I'd be a much better
gnome blacksmith
if they let me have a

bigger hammer...

Sometimes it's nice
to be over a barrel...

Gnome Leaders

Gnomes are democratic and choose their leader (the gnome king) by a series of special votes, followed by a swimsuit competition and a general knowledge round. If there's a tie, they just go for whoever has the biggest beard. The gnome king decides who uses which toadstool and who can fish where. He also enters significant events in the centuries-old gnome tome but spends most of his time perched on a big log with a cup of dandelion wine, laughing uproariously.

59

Popular gnome films:

Gnome Alone,
Gnoman Holiday,
Toadstool Recall.

61

I say, Crispin,
     let's form a motorbicycle gang!
     That'd be absolutely top banana!

Gnome Farming

Gnomes love to grow crops, but it's difficult to do without disturbing the existing grass and flowerbeds. So they get very good at "stealth farming" – hiding fruit and vegetables anywhere they can. If you look closely in your own garden, maybe you'll spot tiny turnips amongst your tulips, or itty-bitty corn dotted around your lawn. Sometimes gnomes will hitch a passing cat to a plough, although that tends to create a rather erratic path over fences and up onto roofs.

63

You have no idea how time consuming it is sweeping an entire garden!

I've been at it for years!

64

You're my best mate,
Mr Squirrel.

Let's start our
own patisserie.

This golden acorn will help.

Gnome Sailors

Apart from the occasional octopus's garden, the seabed is not usually a suitable location for a gnomic residence. However, a surprising number of gnomes have opted for a sailor's life. Although few boats come with grass, ponds or toadstools, a gnome's positive view of the world can find the arboreal just about anywhere. The masts are trees, the deck is the lawn and their fellow shipmates' colourful tattoos form the flowerbeds. And they can always do their fishing off the side!

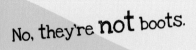

No, they're **not** boots.

My feet actually are **THAT** hairy.

68

I say,
this is an
absolutely
super book!

wish I could read!

Must think about the deep mysteries of life, for example:

How do they get ships into bottles?

And more importantly, **why?**

Gnome Singing

Gnomes have beautiful, sweet singing voices – each one is totally unique. They love to form close harmony groups and hold singalongs. They have even been known to charm the birds from the trees and attract a huge crowd of entranced forest animals. A common concern is that humans will hear them and come out of their houses, scaring the animals; even worse, that people might catch the gnomes in a big net and force them to appear on a TV talent show where third-rate celebrities would make snide remarks about their pointy hats. For this reason gnomes use their special powers to block the sound from entering people's homes. Either that or they use a lot of leftover egg cartons to make soundproof walls.

Are you sure I shouldn't just go to a dentist?

There's not a lot of work for the gnome police!

Just the occasional toadstool dispute, a rowdy party or some tax fraud or other.

Gnome
Basket weaving

Gnomes need baskets for carrying all kinds of things, from laundry to tiny crops, so many gnomes are trained in the ancient art of weaving. With just a bit of straw or indeed any other sturdy stalk, a blur of tiny gnomish fingers can create an amazing holdall. A lot of the baskets you find in the shops were made by gnome artisans and discarded because they are too big for gnomes to use. The biggest gnome basket weaving achievement was the notorious wicker submarine project. The resulting vessel was surprisingly waterproof but rendered unusable when the periscope was bitten off by a passing goat.

Although gnomes are often seen

with fishing rods, they are all

vegetarians so are probably just

hoping that someone has dumped

a piece of tofu in the pond.

This also explains
why many of their
favourite ponds don't
have any fish.

Gnote this gnome's anguish at having accidentally caught a fish.

Hey, I'm a gnome gninja!

You didn't see me behind these flowers did you?

You did? Oh, frogs.

Gnomes and Flower Shows

There has been some controversy in recent years over the banning of Gnomes from a number of high profile flower shows. While the usual excuse is that their presence is in some way "tacky" or distracting, the truth is somewhat more startling: gnomes in fact run the flower shows and feel it would be too ostentatious if they also featured in them.

81

Gnome hypnotism!

People really will believe anything, won't they...?

Mm mumble...

Back off, Sherlock Holmes...
That's not **your** cheesecake!

zzzZzzzzZzzZZ

83

Gnomes and Animals

Animals frequently act as guardians for gnomes, watching over them and making sure they are safe. Frogs and squirrels in particular enjoy excellent relations with gnomes. The former love the dampness of ponds and toadstools, and the latter are rewarded for their help with nuts that gnomes gather for them in their spare time. Birds also keep a beady lookout from the trees, although that can be quite tricky because gnomes all look pretty much the same from above (like a row of little red tents). Who on earth would want to be mean to a gnome, you ask? Our studies have so far been unable to establish the gnature of the gnome's enemy but we suspect goblins since they always seem to be up to something, don't they?

85

WOW,
I'm really living
high on the hog now!

I remember when I first caught you, Mr Fish.

That was great.

Lucky you can breathe out of water, eh?

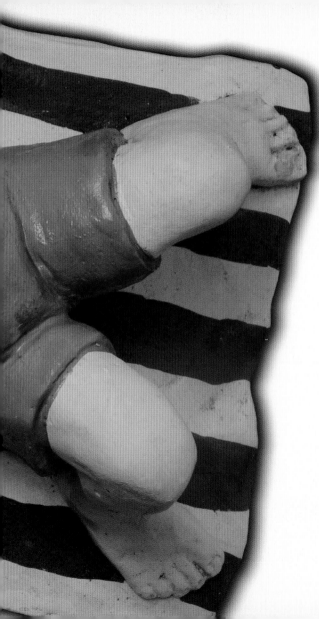

Gnomes and Weather

Since gnomes spend pretty much all of their time outdoors, they have developed a number of coping strategies for different types of weather. If it rains heavily, they hide under toadstools, trees or badgers. When it's foggy and they can't see each other, they whistle special identifying tunes or just nick a torch from the inside of your house. Snow makes them go crazy – they build little snow gnomes and have snowball fights that somehow last for days, long after the snow has melted. During a sunny spell, gnomes just relax and bask in the solar energy. They usually slap on factor 5000 sunscreen, though, since they burn easily and don't want to end up looking like little beetroots.

I tell you Miss Ladybird, it's been a tough day...

pretending to fish, pushing a wheelbarrow,

helping people cheat at cards...

Zzzz.

This is the most literal game of leapfrog ever.

91

Gnomes are great **philosophers**

since they have a lot of time to think
and stroke their big white beards

(which, incidentally, are full of food particles).

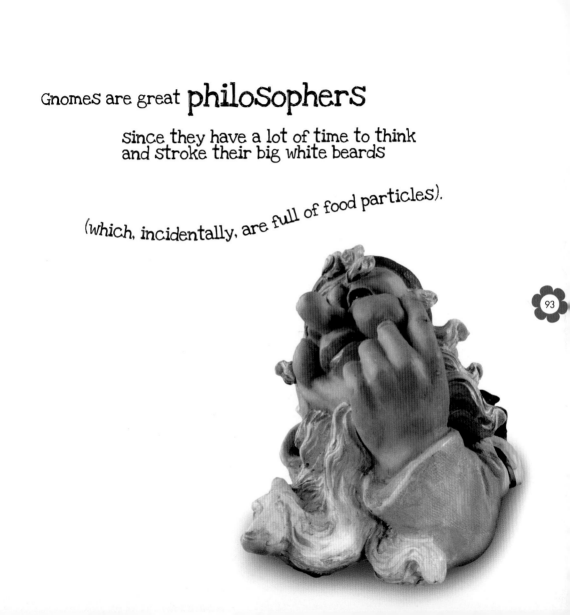

No, I'm not Father Christmas,
but thanks anyway!

Always nice to have people sit on my lap.

Nobody ever sits on my lap...
Say I Smell of old cabbage...

mumble grumble.

GNOME HOMES

Gnomes live in lots of different places. While some clearly just like to stay outdoors, others like nothing better than to snuggle down of an evening in their own little front room and watch the telly. They make their homes in shoes, boxes, super-sized toadstools and pine cones, logs, statues and bushes. If you see an unusually large replica of a garden gnome there's a strong possibility it might have a family of six real gnomes living inside it! Don't try to check though as that would be rude.

Keep making jokes like that, Cedric, and I will tie you up again.

99

And you said we couldn't make a set of bijou studio apartments from a manky old log!

In your face, Squirrel!

Geoff, you'll find it works better if you actually start it up.

103

This pipe is huge!
I don't ever light it,
just in case it starts
a beard fire...

104

ROBOGNOME!
Half gnome,
half tractor,
all awesome!

Just kidding...

105

Gnomes and Us

Hopefully, what you've learned from this book is that gnomes and humankind have a great affinity with each other – one that should be nurtured as they have a lot to teach us and we have a lot of stuff they can borrow when we're out. In gnome society there is no longer any war, hatred or suffering. But there's no deep-pan pizza either, so maybe we're one up from them on that. If you haven't already done so, feel encouraged to make your garden a gnome-friendly zone. Put in a little pond, dart some toadstools about the place, put up a few signs like "Gnomes Welcome" or "Homes For Gnomes Here" and see what happens. You're bound to be pleasantly surprised.

Favourite gnome
ice cream flavours:

Gnomeapolitan,
Toadstool Ripple,
Rocky Toad.

So when you said you carried a torch for me,

you meant that literally!

Remember this:
no matter where you go, there's always a gnome right behind you.

I thought that was lovely.

Although we didn't tell them the **real** reason
for the pointy hats...